The
Black Dog

by Lynn Trepicchio
illustrated by Neil Posis

Printed in the United States of America

ISBN 0-15-317817-5

Ordering Options
ISBN 0-15-317821-3 (Grade 1 Collection)
ISBN 0-15-319439-1 (package of 5)

3 4 5 6 7 8 9 10 179 2003 2002 2001

I went walking.

Did you see a black
dog?

I saw a yellow dog.

Did you see a black
dog?

I saw a green dog.

I saw a red dog.

I saw a brown dog.

I see a black dog
walking to me!

Teacher/Family Member..

Color Concentration

Make a game with colors and color names. On one set of cards, write the color names. Have children color another set of cards, using the corresponding colors. Spread the cards face down on the table, mix them up, and take turns matching the cards.

 School-Home Connection

Invite your child to read aloud *The Black Dog*. Help him or her read the color words in the story.

Word Count: 43

Vocabulary Words: black
                      brown
                      did
                      green
                      red
                      saw
                      see
                      walking
                      went
                      yellow

Phonic Elements: Consonant: /d/ *d*; Short Vowel: /i/ *i*
                      did

TAKE-HOME BOOK
Together Again
Use with "I Went Walking."